TITLE IX ROCKS!
PLAY LIKE A GIRL™

TENNIS
GIRLS ROCKING IT

NITA MALLICK and JUDITH GUILLERMO-NEWTON

NEW YORK

Published in 2016 by The Rosen Publishing Group, Inc.
29 East 21st Street, New York, NY 10010

Copyright © 2016 by The Rosen Publishing Group, Inc.

First Edition

All rights reserved. No part of this book may be reproduced in any form without permission in writing from the publisher, except by a reviewer.

Library of Congress Cataloging-in-Publication Data

Mallick, Nita.
 Tennis : girls rocking it / Nita Mallick and Judith Guillermo-Newton. — First Edition.
     pages cm. — ((Title IX rocks! Play like a girl))
 Includes bibliographical references and index.
 Audience: Grades: 7-12.
 ISBN 978-1-5081-7041-9 (Library bound)
 1. Tennis for girls—Juvenile literature. I. Guillermo-Newton, Judith. II. Title.
 GV1001.4.G57M35 2016
 796.342082–dc23

                                                            2015025482

Manufactured in China

CONTENTS

04 INTRODUCTION

08 CHAPTER ONE
TENNIS BASICS

19 CHAPTER TWO
TENNIS TRAINING

28 CHAPTER THREE
THE COMPETITIVE SPIRIT

35 CHAPTER FOUR
LEADING LIGHTS OF WOMEN'S TENNIS: PIONEERS AND CHAMPIONS

48 CHAPTER FIVE
GET IN THE GAME!

53 TIMELINE

56 GLOSSARY

58 FOR MORE INFORMATION

61 FOR FURTHER READING

63 INDEX

INTRODUCTION

The Civil Rights Act of 1964 was a landmark piece of legislation, signed into law by President Lyndon B. Johnson, that made discrimination in various fields on the basis of race, color, national origin, and religious affiliation illegal. In the area of employment, the act forbade gender-based discrimination, though it neglected to address similar discrimination in public education. This omission would be corrected eight years later by President Richard M. Nixon, when he signed into law the U.S. Education Amendments of 1972, a set of statutes meant to clarify or expand some aspects of the earlier Civil Rights Act. At the signing ceremony, President Nixon mainly discussed the amendments' impact upon the then contentious issue of busing. The government was attempting to desegregate public schools by busing students to school districts other than their own. Left unmentioned was one particular amendment, officially named Title IX of the Education Amendments of 1972, but popularly known simply as Title IX.

Signed into federal law, Title IX prohibits discrimination on the basis of sex in any federally funded education program or activity. It states that "No person in the United States shall, on the basis of sex, be excluded from participation in, be denied the benefits of, or be subjected to discrimination under any education program or activity receiving federal financial assistance." The principal objective of Title IX is

Thanks to Title IX, high schools and colleges around the United States offer a variety of athletics programs—including tennis—for girls and women.

to avoid the use of federal money to support sex discrimination in education programs and to provide individual citizens protection against such discrimination. Title IX applies, with a few specific exceptions, to all aspects of federally funded education programs or activities. In addition to traditional educational institutions such as colleges, universities, and elementary and secondary schools, Title IX also applies to any education or training program operated by a recipient of federal financial assistance.

Critics and supporters alike initially focused upon the ways in which Title IX would impact issues like nondiscriminatory hiring and employment practices and equal access to quality education, facilities, and extracurricular activities in public educational and federally financed institutions. It soon became apparent, however, that Title IX would also revolutionize women's athletics. Under Title IX, public educational institutions would have to provide a selection of sports and levels of competition that served the interests and abilities of both sexes. There would have to be a rough equality of funding for and provision of athletic equipment, supplies, facilities, publicity, and scholarships relating to men's and women's athletics. Up to this time, women were significantly underrepresented in high school and college athletics, and funding for female athletics was a small fraction of what was spent on male athletics. This was all about to change dramatically.

One of the first people to recognize the revolutionary power of Title IX and its transformative potential for girls and women was the professional tennis champion Billie Jean King. From day one, she was a powerful supporter of and vocal advocate for Title IX's vital importance to increasing women's participation in and equal access to athletics. She recognized its ability to transform society's perception of what was appropriate activity for women and what women were capable of achieving. While fighting against staunch resistance to get Title IX implemented, King also fought a parallel fight for equality within the ranks of professional tennis. One year after the passage of Title IX, King spearheaded the formation of the

INTRODUCTION

Women's Tennis Association (WTA), a players' union that, among many other things, fought successfully to gain tournament prize winnings that were equal to those awarded to male tennis players. That same year, 1973, King offered a vivid illustration of women's equality in athletics by soundly defeating the former tennis champion Bobby Riggs, who had boasted that he could beat any of the top female players.

Thanks to King and other supporters of equality in female athletics, the landscape has been profoundly altered. In 1972, just one in twenty-seven girls participated in high school varsity sports. Today, about two in five girls participate as a result of the legislation. In women's collegiate programs, there has been an increase in participation of over 500 percent. Current champions like Serena and Venus Williams and Maria Sharapova are the beneficiaries of Title IX and are inspiring and triumphant examples of its positive effects.

Women's tennis is regarded as being at the vanguard of progress towards athletic equality, the frontrunner among sports as regards equality of access, opportunity, achievement, and funding. It also happens to be a fast-paced and exciting game, dependent upon speed, skill, and strategy. What better way to celebrate the legacy of Title IX and the equality fought so hard for by pioneering heroes like Billie Jean King than to pick up a racket and hit the courts?

TENNIS BASICS

The origins of tennis are shrouded in mystery and speculation. The game we know today may be the descendant of ancient ball games played by the Egyptians, Greeks, and Romans. Some historians of the sport believe it comes from a Roman game called harpastum, a cross between football and rugby, in which two teams fought each other to get the ball over a line marked at each end of the field. What is known for certain, however, is that tennis has been played in England at least since the 1500s, during the reign of King Henry VIII, and was brought to the eastern United States in the late 1800s. It was often referred to as lawn tennis because matches were played on grass courts. The United States National Lawn Tennis Association formed in 1884 and that year sponsored a national championship in men's singles and doubles. In 1887, women's singles was added, and in 1890, women's doubles rounded out the tournament.

TENNIS BASICS

Dorothea Douglass (later Dorothea Lambert Chambers) was a leading British tennis champion in the pre–World War I era—a time when tennis was still a largely male-dominated sport.

Tennis was then a sport of the wealthy. Like golf, it was part of the culture of private clubs that excluded African Americans, Jews, and recent immigrants. It wasn't until the mid-twentieth century that many Jewish tennis clubs and the all-black American Tennis Association were established.

Today, tennis is accessible to everyone. Over 160,000 public tennis courts exist around the United States. Some cities charge adults for public court use, but virtually all public courts are free to children. Membership in private tennis clubs is often expensive, but many clubs do have special tennis membership rates available for junior tennis players (student-age players, from eight to eighteen years old).

The basic requirements for a tennis game include a tennis racket, tennis balls, tennis shoes, an accessible tennis court, and at least one other person with whom to play. In many cities there are organizations that collect used tennis rackets and make them available to beginning tennis enthusiasts. This is an excellent way to get your start in tennis and see what you think of the sport.

THE EQUIPMENT YOU WILL NEED

For a beginning tennis player, choosing a racket can be very confusing. The tennis racket is used to hit the ball over the net and consists of a frame, which may be of any weight, size, or shape, and stringing. It can be made of wood, graphite, titanium, or other materials.

A shop specializing in tennis equipment can help you decide which racket is best for you. In choosing a racket, it is vital to get

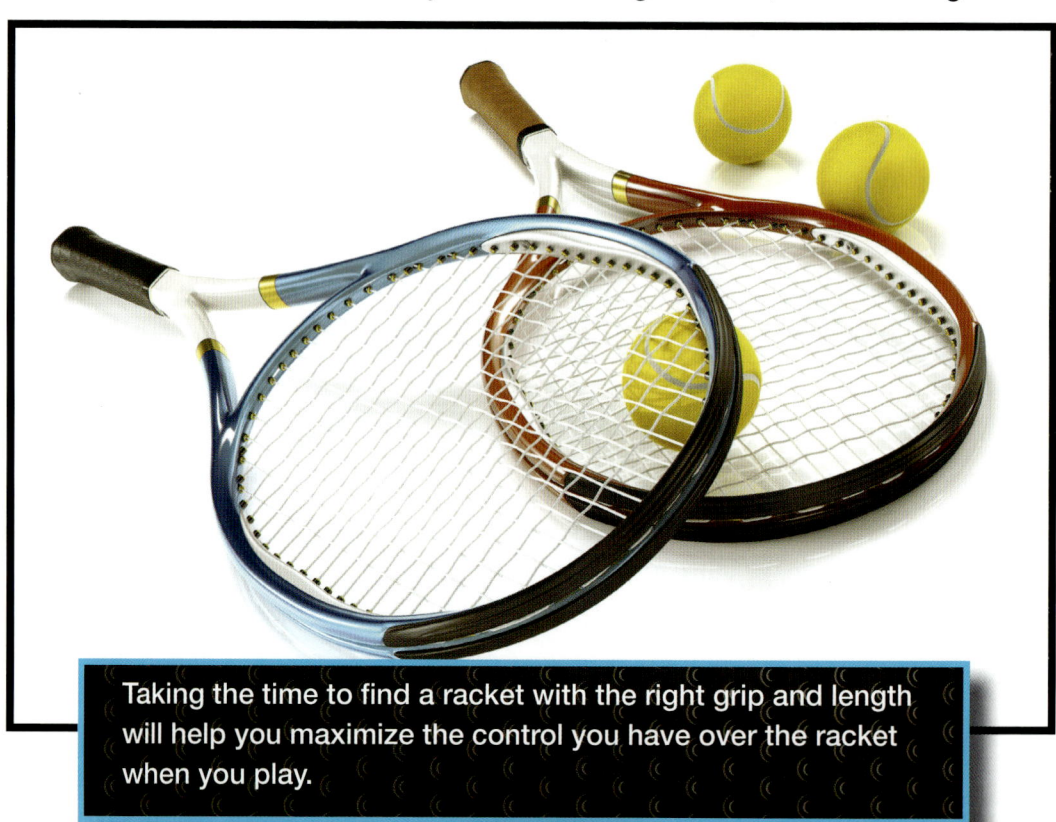

Taking the time to find a racket with the right grip and length will help you maximize the control you have over the racket when you play.

the correct grip (handle) size. To determine grip size, take the racket by the end of the handle as if you were going to shake hands. Close your fingers around the grip; there should be one finger's width of space between your thumb and index finger.

To play tennis, you also need a can of balls. Tennis balls are usually sold three to a can. Most tennis balls are yellow or white, and they are made up of a pressurized rubber core covered with high-quality cloth, usually wool mixed with nylon. With play, tennis balls gradually go soft and need to be replaced. When tennis balls go soft, they're referred to as dead balls. Playing with dead balls can cause you to strain and injure your elbow.

TENNIS APPAREL

Most public courts do not have a strict dress code. The only rule usually refers to tennis shoes; players must use soft-sole rubber shoes that do not leave marks on the court surface. This usually means no black-sole tennis shoes. Playing tennis can be hard on your feet. Good tennis shoes are essential for preventing injuries because they support the foot and absorb shock. There are shoes designed especially for tennis, but if you play only occasionally, or play several sports, you can use a pair of cross-trainers.

Private tennis courts often have specific dress codes. This usually means all white clothes, tennis skirts for women, and tennis shorts for men, though some clubs have more relaxed rules. It is a good idea to check if the court on which you are playing has a dress code.

THE SCORING SYSTEM

To win a tennis game, a player must win four points and win by a margin of two. The scoring progresses from 15 to 30 to 40 to game.

TENNIS

ON THE COURT

The dimensions of a tennis court are 78 feet by 27 feet (23.8 meters by 8.2 meters) for singles (one-on-one play) and 78 feet by 36 feet (23.8 m by 11 m) for doubles (when teams of two play one another). The net, located midcourt, is three feet (1 m) high in the center. At each side where it is supported by posts, the net stands three and a half feet (1.07 m) high. Although grass courts are still in use, the most common court materials today are clay,

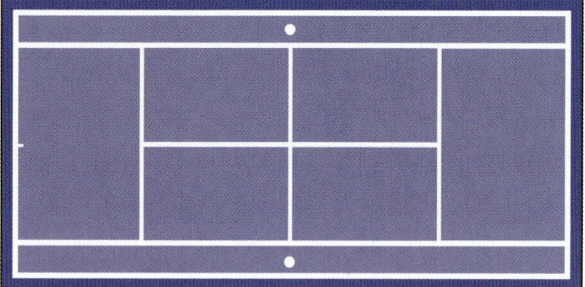

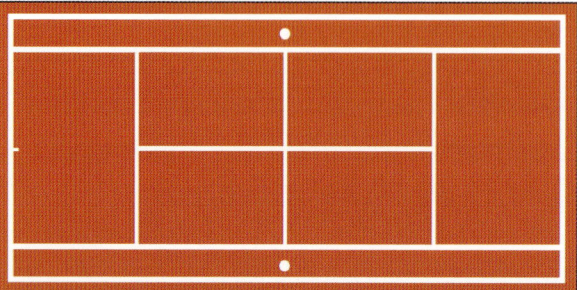

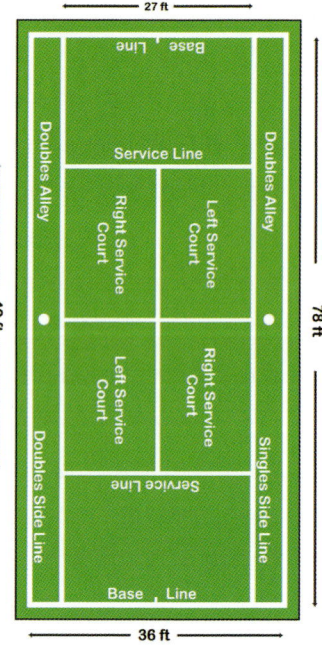

Hard courts (*top left*), clay courts (*bottom left*), and grass courts (*right*) have the same dimensions. However, the different surfaces affect ball speed and strategy.

12

cement, and a number of cushioned asphalt and synthetic surfaces. These are usually referred to as hard courts.

If you are playing doubles, you use the entire width of the tennis court. If you are playing singles, the inside vertical line, or alley line, designates your court. The service line is the horizontal line 18 feet (5.5 m) from the back line of the court (the baseline). It is the start of the service court. The service court is divided in the center into right and left service courts. The area between the service line and the baseline is referred to as the backcourt.

If you are tied at 40-40, this is called deuce. If the server wins the next point, the score is referred to as advantage-in, or ad-in. If she wins the next point, the server wins by two points, and the game is over. If the receiver wins the next point after deuce, the score is advantage-out, or ad-out. A player always has to win by two points for the game to be over. There is no limit to the number of deuce points that can be played in a game.

When calling out the score, the server's score is always reported first: the score 30-15 means that the server has won two points and the receiver has won one. One person serves an entire game. In tennis, zero is generally referred to as "love," from the French word l'oeuf, which means "egg" (just as English speakers sometimes use the term "goose egg" to refer to zero). The score love-40 tells us the server has no points and the receiver has three.

A player loses the point by missing the ball, hitting it into the net, or hitting it out of bounds. A server loses the point immediately if she commits a double fault—failing to hit the ball in the service box after two tries.

As points make up a game, games make up a set, and sets make up a match. The first player to win six games wins the set, but a player must be two games ahead to win. Therefore, a set could be won at 7-5. If the set score ends at 6-6, the players either play a tiebreaker or continue to play until one person is ahead by two games. To win a match, a player must win two out of three sets. From 1984–1998, players had to win three out of five sets to win the WTA championship. Men play best of five sets in Grand Slam tournaments.

THE ART OF THE SERVE

For most beginning players, the serve is the most difficult and frustrating tennis skill to learn. This is the shot used by players to begin a point. The actual motion used to hit the ball is referred to as the service motion. To be a legitimate serve, the tennis ball must cross the net, without touching it, and land crosscourt in the service box on the opposite side of the net. If the ball touches the net and bounces into the service box, this is called a let, and the server gets another try. The server is allowed two tries to get the ball legally into play. If a ball does not land in the server's box, this is called a fault. If she is not successful on either of the two attempts, this is called a double fault, and she loses the point.

Service starts on the right side of the court (the deuce court). The server must stand behind the baseline anywhere between the center hash mark and the alley line. After the point is completed, the server moves to the left side of the court (the ad court) and serves diagonally across the court once again.

TENNIS BASICS

Perfecting a serve may take some time, but knowing how to start the game off right is key to a good match.

THE VOLLEY SHOT

The volley is a type of tennis shot made while the player is standing close to the net. With a short, punching motion, the player tries to hit the ball in the air before it bounces. When hitting a volley, the player wants to stand about three feet (0.9 m) from the net with her feet spread apart about shoulder-width. The racket strings should be perpendicular to the ground, and the racket should be directly in front of her. The bottom of the handle should be even with the belly button. When the ball crosses the net, the player wants to meet it with a short jab-like stroke.

GROUNDSTROKES: FOREHAND AND BACKHAND

A groundstroke is a tennis stroke generally hit by a player from the baseline. When both players stand at or behind the baseline to hit balls back and forth to one another, this is a baseline rally.

The forehand is one of two basic groundstrokes. If a player is right-handed and hits the ball on her right side, this tennis stroke is called a forehand. If the player is left-handed and hits the ball on her left side, this is her forehand. The ball strikes the racket on the front of the strings.

The backhand, in which the ball hits the backside of the tennis racket, is the other basic groundstroke of tennis. If a player is right-handed, a ball hit on the left side of her body would be a backhand. (The reverse is true for left-handers.) To hit the ball, she has to cross her body with the hand holding the racket. Much more commonly than in the forehand stroke, the backhand can be hit with one or two hands holding the racket. The backhand often takes longer to master than the forehand.

TENNIS BASICS

Many advanced players work their way up to a one-handed backhand, but learning a two-handed backhand is important at all skill levels, from beginner to professional.

Below are some basic tips for how to begin perfecting your forehand and backhand and increasing their power.

Forehand Tips

- Always pull the racket back as soon as the ball is approaching your forehand side.
- Try to hit the ball on the sweet spot (middle area) of the racket.
- When hitting the ball, keep your feet spread about shoulder-width apart.
- Step toward the ball with your right foot if you're right-handed, your left foot if you're left-handed.

- Continue your stroke after you've hit the ball so that your racket head follows through the ball toward your opposite shoulder.

Backhand Tips

- As the ball is hit toward you, turn your shoulders to the left if you are right-handed, to the right if you are left-handed. Your back will be to the net.
- When hitting the ball, keep your head very still. Follow the ball with your eyes only.
- When hitting the ball, keep your feet spread about shoulder-width apart.
- Finish the shot up and over the right shoulder (opposite if you are left-handed).

TENNIS TRAINING

Those who are unfamiliar with tennis may incorrectly believe that it is a casual, laid-back sport, in which players lazily lob the ball back and forth at one another, with a minimum of effort, motion, or strategy. Nothing could be further from the truth. Tennis is a high-energy, high-intensity, highly demanding contest of wit, wiles, and athleticism of the highest order.

Aerobic activities, strength training, and stretching will get a person in the necessary condition for tennis. Tennis is a game of quick motions, stopping and starting, and sudden surges at maximum speed. Playing tennis improves flexibility in the joints, primarily in the hips and the shoulders, which are used in the serving motion. Tennis also develops and tones one's muscles, especially the biceps and triceps in the arms; calves, hamstrings, and quadriceps in the legs; and deltoids and rhomboid in the shoulders and upper back

All players will improve their cardiovascular fitness, but as one's skill level improves, workouts become more intense, partly because the points take longer to play. As players improve, they can move their opponents around the court more, which also makes tennis an active aerobic workout.

STRETCHING AND WARMING UP

The more fit you are, the better your chances of reducing the risk of injury. It is very important to warm up for at least five to ten minutes before playing tennis; this small amount of effort can greatly reduce your chances of getting hurt. A good warm-up is to come to the net and gently hit the ball back and forth to another player. This should get your muscles warm and your eyes focusing on the ball. As your muscles get loose, you can then move to the baseline and hit groundstrokes.

In order to prevent injury, be sure to stretch the major muscle groups after you warm up but before beginning play or practice in earnest. Stretch again after playing or practicing to promote flexibility and prevent unnecessary soreness the next day. The muscles you should concentrate on warming up and "cooling down" (after play or practice) are the calves, gluteus muscles, hamstrings, quadriceps, triceps, and muscles of the shoulders and upper and lower back.

To boost your agility, try running sideways from sideline to sideline, sprinting forward from the baseline to the net, and running backward from the net back to the baseline. To work on your hand-eye coordination, practice hitting against a backboard or with a ball machine, or play softball, ping pong, racquetball, or squash. Also work on strengthening your arms and lower back, two of the areas most often injured in tennis.

TENNIS TRAINING

Most experts recommend doing static stretching (stretching muscles while you're not moving), such as this quadriceps stretch, only after warming up.

TAKING LESSONS

Tennis is a game in which receiving formal lessons can be extremely helpful, both in the early stages of learning the game and in order to continue to improve. It is very easy to develop bad habits that can limit your progress as well as cause injury.

Good tennis instruction is available from many different places. The YMCA and most public tennis courts or city recreation programs offer affordable tennis lessons. Group tennis lessons are the least expensive way to get formal instruction. This is also an easy way to meet other people at your level with whom to play tennis. Private tennis clubs and private professionals also offer tennis instruction, but the cost is usually much higher than that of public recreation programs. The one-on-one instruction and individual

A good instructor can help you understand how to capitalize on your strengths and what areas you should work on improving.

attention they offer, however, can be well worth the money and can result in more rapid progress and improvement.

The United States Tennis Association (USTA) offers many tennis programs in different areas around the country. They are easily accessed online at www.USTA.com. Other tennis sites also list different tennis camps available throughout the world.

TENNIS LINGO

ACE A legal serve that the receiver doesn't touch.
ADVANTAGE (AD) COURT The left side of the court for each player.
APPROACH SHOT The transition shot that allows a player to get from the baseline area to the net. This can be hit off the forehand and backhand sides.
CENTER HASH MARK A line that divides each side of the court in half and is crucial to the serving game.
CHANGEOVER Players must change ends of the court when the games add up to an odd number. This keeps the match fair so that both players must face elements such as the wind, sun, and shade.
DEUCE When the score is tied at 40-40. If the server wins the next point, it is called advantage in; if the receiver wins, it is called advantage out. The player with the advantage must win the next point to win the game.
DEUCE COURT The right side of the court for each player.

(continued on the next page)

(continued from the previous page)

DOUBLES ALLEY Long, narrow rectangles created by the singles and doubles sidelines running parallel with each other. These alleys are used only in doubles play.

DOWN THE LINE Down one of the sidelines. A shot down the line is a lower percentage shot because the net is higher and the ball doesn't travel as far.

FIRST SERVE At the beginning of each point, the server has two chances to get the serve in. The first serve is usually the harder serve.

FOOT FAULT Occurs if the server touches or crosses the baseline with either foot before the ball is hit.

LET A call by the umpire for a do-over of a serve. Usually, this happens if the serve touches the net before landing in a legal spot of the court.

RETURN OF SERVE The shot made by a player when receiving the serve.

TIEBREAKER At 6-all in games, in any given set, players must play a tiebreaker. The first player to reach 7 by a margin of 2 is the winner. The points are counted as 1, 2, 3 . . . and so on. A tiebreaker can go on until someone eventually wins by two points, such as 18-16.

WINNING THE TOSS One player spins her racket or tosses a coin to see who gets choice of either serve or side of the court, not both. If you choose to serve, then the opponent chooses which side of the court she wants first.

PREVENTING COMMON TENNIS INJURIES

A crucial reason to take tennis lessons is that learning the proper way to hit a stroke is the best insurance you can have against injury. Warming up and stretching both before and after you play tennis also helps. The most common tennis injuries are to the feet, ankles, knees, elbows, and shoulders.

The feet probably take more abuse than any other part of the human body. They not only support the entire body, but they also act as shock absorbers. The feet are responsible for keeping our bodies balanced as we quickly stop and start on the tennis court. Side-to-side movement and the hard surfaces of the tennis court are fatiguing to the feet and can make them susceptible to injury. Injured feet can, in turn, contribute to ankle and knee injuries.

It is common to feel muscle soreness after you play. However, if you are injured or notice unusual pain or discomfort in your body, consult a doctor before playing again.

Properly fitting tennis shoes are absolutely essential for keeping your feet in good shape. They not only offer arch support, but they also help absorb the pounding you get from playing on hard courts. The fit of your shoes is important because excessive friction between the shoe and the skin can cause blisters. Socks that are thin or don't breathe can also cause blisters. Poorly fitting footwear can cause calluses to form on your feet. Calluses are thick, hardened patches of dead skin cells that form over areas of bone pressure, usually on the ball or heel of the foot. For people who have weak ankles, high-top tennis shoes can be helpful in preventing injuries.

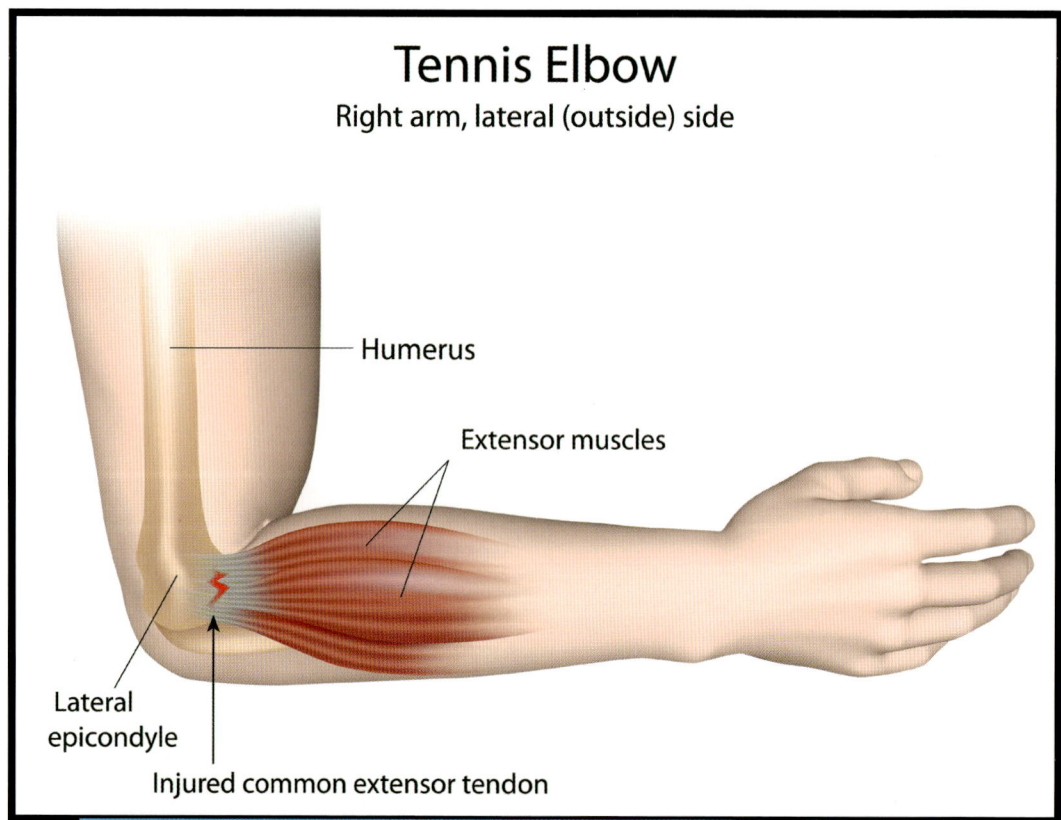

Tennis Elbow
Right arm, lateral (outside) side

- Humerus
- Extensor muscles
- Lateral epicondyle
- Injured common extensor tendon

Tennis elbow is usually treatable. If you think you might be affected, give your arm a rest and consult a medical professional.

An alarming number of female athletes report injuries to their knees' anterior cruciate ligaments, or ACL, the elastic-like bands that connect the shins and thigh bones. Researchers say running backward can help build hamstring muscles. Bending the knees when playing tennis can also help reduce ACL injuries.

The most common cause of elbow pain in tennis players is a tendon problem known as tendonitis (an irritation or irritation of the elbow tendon that attaches muscle to bone). In fact, this condition is so common to tennis players that it's called tennis elbow. The usual causes are poor technique, most commonly on your backhand stroke, or using a racket with the wrong grip size. This is yet another reason to have a tennis professional help you choose the proper racket and teach you how to correctly hit a ball.

THE COMPETITIVE SPIRIT

The idea of competition can be difficult for many girls. Some of us are uncomfortable with the idea that girls can be as competitive as boys. We see compeition as a "male thing." But many girls love to compete; they are driven by the idea of excelling and of winning. They want to be the best at whatever it is they are doing, be it tennis, soccer, dance, or debate. They receive great pleasure from entering the competition, challenging others, and seeing themselves succeed. You can be a passionate competitor, especially in sports, and not have to apologize for it.

For those who aren't competitive by nature, remember that it is okay to win. If you beat someone else, it does not make you a bad person. Shape competition into a game in which the goal is to give your personal best regardless of the result. Many athletes let competition take the fun out of the sport. It is important to remember

THE COMPETITIVE SPIRIT

You don't have to be competitive to enjoy tennis, though competition can be great motivation for some to improve or excel. However, it never excuses poor sportsmanship.

that when we try our hardest and we lose, we are not losers—we merely lost a game.

A WINNING ATTITUDE

Tennis is as much a game of the mind as it is of the body. The mental game consists of staying focused and not getting distracted. It

Serena Williams won the U.S. Open trophy in 2014 for the fifth time. Not only is she an exceptional tennis player, she is a gracious competitor.

means talking positively to yourself and staying composed even when things are not working in your favor. It means forgiving yourself when you make a mistake and encouraging yourself to do better.

Serena Williams is widely considered the best tennis player, man or woman, to ever play the game. Most tennis players peak when they are young and remain champions for only a few short years. Williams won her first Grand Slam tournament (the four Grand

EMBRACE VICTORY!

In her book *Embracing Victory*, Mariah Burton Nelson, an award-winning author and athlete, offers a view of competition she refers to as a partnership model. Nelson looks at power not as "power over" (dominating power) but as "power to" (power as competence). She sees teammates, coaches, and even opposing players viewing each other as comrades rather than enemies. She proposes that these "comrades" help us to find the best in ourselves by challenging us and pushing us to do better.

Nelson also talks about the need for women to feel comfortable about taking up space with their bodies and their voices, conveying their ideas, asserting their own needs, and refusing to shrink to meet someone's approval. Billie Jean King offers an insightful endorsement of this point of view: "In the

(continued on the next page)

TENNIS

(continued from the previous page)

Respecting your opponents and treating them as comrades who have common interests as you is a good way to build a healthy attitude toward them and the game.

'70s, many of us, myself included, were outrageous and cutting-edge. But in my generation we also tried to please…[T]hese young women [current female professional tennis players] certainly are showing their self confidence. If they had been boys or young men, everyone would have expected it. It's a fine line, but I like the fact that these girls have higher self-esteem and they're not afraid to show it"

Slam events are the U.S. Open, the French Open, Wimbledon, and the Australian Open) in 1999. In 2015, sixteen years later, she won Wimbledon, her 21st career Grand Slam triumph. It was her fourth Grand Slam in a row, making her the reigning champion of all the Grand Slam events. It was the second time she completed a non–calendar year Grand Slam (winning all four tournaments consecutively). She became, at thirty-three, the oldest woman to ever win a Grand Slam tournament.

Triumphing in a sport over such a long time, when the competition keeps getting younger, fresher, and stronger, requires enormous dedication, effort, hard work, resilience, focus, and physical and mental strength and tenacity. When you see Serena Williams on the court, you can feel her intensity of focus. Nothing distracts her; she is completely in the moment, paying attention only to the task at hand, coaching herself between points, focusing intently on positive thoughts, and visualizing successful outcomes.

Win or lose, Williams is gracious to her opponents. And, after losing efforts, she is forgiving to herself but resolves to identify and fix those parts of her game that were weak. In 2015, she was poised to become only the fourth tennis player to achieve a calendar-year Grand Slam if she won the U.S. Open. Despite high hopes, she lost a semifinal match to competitor Roberta Vinci. Still, Williams had kind words for the victor, calling her "inspiring." To the 2015 U.S. Open winner, Flavia Pennetta, Williams tweeted, "I'm so happy you won. You deserved it."

WIN OR LOSE, HAVE FUN AND BELIEVE IN YOURSELF

Few players thrive on negativity or pressure. The key is to have fun. Approach problems as a puzzle you can enjoy solving. Look for patterns. Try new strategies or techniques if what you are

Competition doesn't have to be all seriousness. Whether you're playing on a team or on your own, make sure that you're having fun.

doing is not working. Don't let adversity get the better of you. Give your very best and take pride in the effort you put forth. Look at your losses as learning experiences and think about where you can improve. Many coaches say they learn more from their losses than they do from their wins. Most important, believe in yourself; see yourself as a winner, both on and off the court. Remember that self-esteem comes from working at something and getting better at it. Allow playing tennis to enhance your self-esteem, not destroy it.

CHAPTER FOUR

LEADING LIGHTS OF WOMEN'S TENNIS: PIONEERS AND CHAMPIONS

It is believed that a woman named Mary Ewing Outerbridge first introduced tennis to the United States in 1874, using equipment brought over from Bermuda and used on a court she built at her Staten Island home. Indoor tennis was first played in New York City, at the 7th Regiment Armory, where twelve courts were reserved for use by female players. In 1884, Wimbledon added the first Women's Singles championship to its tennis competitions. The first U.S. Open Women's Singles championship was played in 1887 and won by Ellen Hansell. At the dawn of the 20th century, in 1900, women first competed in the Olympic Games. One of the three sports open to the nineteen female athletes was tennis, and it was the most popular with spectators.

Since these early beginnings, women's tennis has come a long way, and the sport's history is filled with a captivating, inspiring

Women's tennis matches draw huge crowds. Here, a captive audience watches player Eugenie Bouchard square off against an opponent at the 2014 Wimbledon tournament.

and powerful roster of champions who demonstrate determination, courage, pride, and achievement both on the court and off.

ALTHEA GIBSON

National and international tennis champion Althea Gibson challenged both other tennis athletes and the racial segregation of tennis that was part of the social structure of the United States in the 1950s.

Born to sharecropper parents in South Carolina on August 27, 1927, the African American Gibson grew up in poverty in Harlem. She enjoyed most sports but adored tennis. In 1942, when Gibson was fifteen years old, she won the girls' singles event at the American Tennis Association's New York State Tournament. The ATA was an all-black tennis organization, because African Americans were not allowed to take part in tournaments with white players.

But Althea Gibson would not be discouraged. In 1951, she became the first African American of either sex to be allowed to enter the Forest Hills National Grass Court Championship. She later went on to win Forest Hills, Wimbledon, and the French Open.

Althea Gibson was a woman of much success, courage, and perseverance. Along with her athletic achievements, Gibson should also be recognized as the first African American of either sex to break the color barrier in national and international tournament tennis. Numerous tennis facilities around the country bear her name. Gibson died on September 28, 2003, at the age of seventy-six, in East Orange, New Jersey.

Althea Gibson plays at the 1956 Wimbledon tournament. By the end of her career, she had won eleven Grand Slam events.

BILLIE JEAN KING

Billie Jean (Moffitt) King was born in Long Beach, California, on November 22, 1943. She has done more for women's tennis than any other player.

King won her first of twenty Wimbledon titles in 1961. She captured six singles, ten doubles, and four mixed doubles titles there.

TENNIS

President Barack Obama presents Billie Jean King with the Presidential Medal of Freedom for her enormous cultural contributions on and off the court.

Additionally, she has thirteen U.S. Open victories (four singles, five doubles, and four mixed doubles), four French Open titles (one singles, one doubles, and two mixed doubles), and two Australian Open titles (one singles and one mixed doubles). That makes a total of thirty-nine Grand Slam victories. With twenty-seven major doubles titles, she has been credited with being one of the greatest doubles players in the history of tennis.

In 1971, King was the first woman athlete to win more than $100,000 in one season. Her much-publicized Battle of the Sexes match against male tennis player Bobby Riggs set a record for the largest tennis audience and the largest prize awarded up to that time. And Billie Jean won!

Billie Jean King worked relentlessly for the rights of women players, cofounding the Women's Tennis Association (WTA) in 1974. She retired from competitive singles tennis in 1983 and from doubles competition in 1990. King was inducted into the International Tennis Hall of Fame in 1987. In 2006, the home of the U.S. Open—the USTA National Tennis Center, in New York's Flushing Meadows-Corona Park—was renamed the USTA Billie Jean King National Tennis Center. She was awarded the Presidential Medal of Freedom in 2009 by President Barack Obama and, in 2013, was inducted into the National Gay and Lesbian Sports Hall of Fame. Many of the opportunities open to young women athletes today can be credited to the work done by Billie Jean King.

CHRIS EVERT

Chris Evert, born on December 21, 1954, began taking tennis lessons at the age of five. Her first teacher was her father, who was a professional tennis coach. At the age of thirteen, she became the number one ranked under-fourteen female player in the U.S. Evert made her Grand Slam debut when she appeared in the U.S. Open in 1971, where she lost to Billie Jean King in a semifinal match. Her first Grand Slam victories came in 1974 when she won both the French Open and Wimbledon.

Evert quickly came to dominate women's tennis throughout the mid-1970s, until the emergence of her fiercest rival, Martina Navratilova. From that point on, the two top tennis players were forever entwined in the popular mind, and their battles on the court were both epic and legendary. They were extremely well-matched. Over the course of their careers, Navratilova won forty-three of their matches, while Evert won thirty-seven. They were frequent doubles partners and good friends off the court.

Evert won at least one Grand Slam singles title a year for thirteen consecutive years between 1974 and 1986, a record that has yet to be beaten. Her record in Grand Slam events was 297-38, an astonishing winning percentage and a testament to her consistent excellence. She won eighteen Grand Slam singles tournaments (seven French Opens, six U.S. Opens, three Wimbledons, and two Australian Opens) and three Grand Slam doubles tournaments (two with Navratilova as partner).

LA DIVINE: SUZANNE LENGLEN

Anyone who knew Suzanne Lenglen as a young child would never have imagined that she would become the first great tennis celebrity, a dominant force on the court, or the first female tennis player to ever turn professional. Born on May 24, 1899, in Compiègne, a French town about 45 miles (72 km) north of Paris, Lenglen was a frail child, afflicted with severe asthma. Her father hoped to invigorate both her body and spirits by encouraging her to play tennis. Once he saw that she enjoyed the game and had some talent, he began training her more formally. One of his techniques was to place handkerchiefs at various points around the court, which Suzanne would then try to aim for. More often than not, she succeeded in hitting her targets. He also had her play against talented male players, believing her female peers were not talented enough to challenge her.

Just four years after first taking up a racket, Lenglen was in the finals of the 1914 French Championships. Though she lost this match, she would go on to win the World Hard Court Championships that same year, making her, at the age of fifteen, the youngest winner of a major tennis championship. No one has yet broken this record.

The tennis world was disrupted and put on hold during World War I, but, once peace was restored,

Lenglen established her dominance of the game. Between 1919 and 1925, she won every Wimbledon singles final, with the exception of the 1924 tournament, when, afflicted with jaundice, she was forced to withdraw. From 1920 to 1926, Lenglen won the French Championships singles final six times and the doubles final five times. In the 1920 Olympics, she won gold medals in women's singles and mixed doubles and a bronze in women's doubles.

Lenglen became the first female tennis player to turn pro when, in 1927, she accepted a $50,000 offer from an American businessman named Charles C. Pyle to tour the U.S. and play in a series of matches against a former U.S. champion, Mary K. Browne. Suddenly, the women's matches were the headliners of the tennis tour, eclipsing the previously dominant men's game. Lenglen beat Browne in every one of their thirty-eight matches, but her real achievement was in defending her decision to turn pro.

Previously, tennis was the domain of wealthy amateurs, who were the only players who could afford the hefty entrance fees and private club memberships. Lenglen had struck the first blow for greater equality of access to the game of tennis and its highest levels of achievement, a battle that in many ways continues to this day.

(continued on the next page)

(continued from the previous page)

Lenglen was a master performer with a flair for the dramatic, which made the game more accessible and opened it up to greater mass appeal. Referred to as *La Divine* (the Divine One) by her French fans, her matches were occasionally marked by sharp flashes of anger, racket throwing, or sobbing fits. She often sipped brandy and cognac between sets. And she scandalized the conservative tennis world, accustomed to seeing female players in apparel that covered their entire body, by appearing in a tennis outfit that featured bare forearms and exposed calves. Lenglen singlehandedly made the largely ignored women's game a runaway crowd favorite, creating a lasting interest in women's tennis and opening the door to greater female participation in sports and social acceptance of women's athletics.

Above all, Lenglen was the most skilled and dominant player of her era. She won thirty-one championship titles between 1914 and 1926. Over the course of her career, she won 241 titles, had a 181-match winning streak, and had an almost 98 percent winning percentage. She was ranked number one during at least part of every year from 1921 to 1926. She lost only one match between 1919 to 1926 and lost only two sets during that period. She introduced an athleticism, aggressiveness, and hard-hitting power that was previously unknown in women's tennis but which looked

LEADING LIGHTS OF WOMEN'S TENNIS: PIONEERS AND CHAMPIONS

> far forward to the modern era of Martina Navratilova, Venus and Serena Williams, and Maria Sharapova.
>
> Lenglen was diagnosed with leukemia in June of 1938. In July, she died at the age of thirty-nine. One of the courts at Roland Garros Stadium, home of the French Open, is named for Lenglen, as is the trophy awarded to the winner of the French Open's women's singles competition. Lenglen was inducted into the International Tennis Hall of Fame in 1978.

Evert retired in 1989. She served as president of the Women's Tennis Association from 1975-76 and 1983-91. She was elected into the International Tennis Hall of Fame in 1995. Evert operates her own tennis academy in Florida, writes for *Tennis* magazine, and serves as a tennis commentator for ESPN.

MARTINA NAVRATILOVA

Martina Navratilova was born in Prague on October 18, 1956, in what was then known as Czechoslovakia, a Communist nation, but today is the democratic Czech Republic. Her stepfather was her first tennis instructor, and she was playing regularly by the time she was seven years old. By the time she was fifteen, she was the national tennis champion of Czechoslovakia. In 1975, after losing in the U.S. Open semifinals to Chris Evert, Navratilova applied for asylum in the U.S., stating that she wished to defect from Communist Czechoslovakia. Asylum was granted, and, in 1981, she became a U.S. citizen.

Navratilova was the first female player to focus intensively on fitness and exercise, particularly strength- and cross-training. She was also one of the first to use a fiberglass-graphite composite racquet. Both of these factors contributed to her dominance of tennis from the late 1970s through the 1980s. Navratilova was ranked number one in the world for a total of 332 weeks in singles and a record 237 weeks in doubles. This astonishing run of success makes her the only player in history to have held the top spot in both singles and doubles for over two hundred weeks. She won eighteen Grand Slam singles titles (three Australian Opens, two French Opens, nine Wimbledons, and four U.S. Opens), thirty-one Grand Slam doubles victories, and ten Grand Slam mixed double victories (the last one in 2006 at the U.S. Open). Her nine Wimbledon singles victories are a record, as are her six consecutive Wimbledon triumphs. She is one of only three women to have won all four Grand Slam tournaments in both singles, doubles, and mixed doubles play.

Navratilova was inducted into the International Tennis Hall of Fame in 2000 but didn't stop playing WTA tennis until 2006, the year of her final victory—a mixed doubles win in the finals of the U.S. Open. Navratilova now works as a tennis coach and is an activist for numerous causes, including for charities that benefit underprivileged children, animal rights, and gay rights.

VENUS WILLIAMS

It is widely agreed that Serena Williams, discussed earlier, is the most talented, most dominant tennis player ever, man or woman. Serena cites numerous players, many women, who helped open the door for her, including Zina Garrison (a Grand Slam-winning African American tennis player active in the 1980s and '90s), Althea Gibson, Arthur Ashe (a three-time Gram Slam–winning, world number one African American player)…and her older sister Venus. Born in California on June 17, 1980, Venus moved with her family to Florida so that she and Serena could attend a leading tennis academy. Venus turned pro in 1994, one year before Serena, and she is credited with taking over where Navratilova left off, taking the sheer power and athleticism of women's tennis to a whole new level.

By 2002, Venus was ranked number one in the world in singles—the first African American woman to reach the top in the Open Era (the period beginning after 1968 when amateur and professional players could compete together in all tournaments). Venus would again reach number one twice more in her career. She has seven career Grand Slam singles titles (five Wimbledons and two U.S. Opens), thirteen Grand Slam doubles titles (with Serena as a partner), and two Grand Slam mixed doubles titles. Venus has also won four Olympic gold medals, one in singles and three in doubles.

While both Venus and Serena are powerful competitors, they do not enjoy facing off against each other. During the period when they were both at the top of the standings, however, such contests were not uncommon. Venus has played against Serena in twenty-seven professional matches, winning eleven of them. They have squared off in eight Grand Slam singles finals, with Serena taking six of them. The thirteen Grand Slam doubles victories and three Olympic gold medals they've shared as partners have been far happier occasions for the sisters.

While continuing to play at a very high level more than twenty years after turning pro, continuing to regularly appear within the top twenty-five, Venus has many other interests outside tennis. She earned her bachelor's degree in business administration in 2015 and plans to work toward a master's degree in that subject. She is the chief executive officer of her own interior design firm, V Starr, and she has her own fashion line named EleVen. Venus and Serena are part owners of the Miami Dolphins football team. Venus has also co-authored a book, *Come to Win: Business Leaders, Artists, Doctors, and Other Visionaries on How Sports Can Help You Top Your Profession*, published in 2010.

MARIA SHARAPOVA

Maria Sharapova's pathway to tennis greatness was paved, in part, by tragedy. Her parents, Yuri and Yelena, lived in Gomel, in the Byelorussian Soviet Socialist Republic. Gomel was hit by moderate amounts of radiation following the Chernobyl nuclear disaster in 1986. Sharapova's parents, awaiting the birth of Maria, decided to leave their home to avoid any danger and move to Russia, where Maria was born on April 19, 1987.

Once settled in Sochi, Russia, Sharapova's father became friends with Aleksandr Kafelnikov, whose son Yevgeny would later became Russia's first world number-one-ranked tennis player. Aleksandr gave Maria her first tennis racquet, and she began playing with her father before working with a professional tennis coach. When she was only six years old, Sharapova attracted the attention of none other than Martina Navratilova, who was hosting a tennis clinic in Moscow. Navratilova urged Sharapova's parents to enroll her in one of the leading U.S. tennis schools in Florida.

Using borrowed money, Yuri raised enough cash for Maria and him to make the trip (Yelena wouldn't be able to join them for two years). Once in Florida, Yuri scrambled for any jobs he could find, including dishwashing, to pay for tennis lessons. His hard work and sacrifice paid off, as a major sports agency spotted Maria's talent, signed her up, and began paying for her academy tuition. Maria was only nine years old at this point.

In 2001, at the age of fourteen, Sharapova entered the pro circuit. Her first full pro season was in 2003, and she quickly broke into the top fifty. By 2004, she had cracked the top twenty. That same year, she won her first Grand Slam singles tournament, defeating defending champion Serena Williams at Wimbledon. "Maria Mania" was born, and there was no looking back. In all, Sharapova has

LEADING LIGHTS OF WOMEN'S TENNIS: PIONEERS AND CHAMPIONS

Becoming a top-ranked player for the first time at just eighteen years old, Maria Sharapova has continued to have a successful tennis career, despite sustaining various injuries.

won five Grand Slam singles tournaments (one Australian Open, one Wimbledon, one U.S. Open, and two French Opens), as well as a silver medal in the 2012 Olympics. Sharapova has been ranked number one in the world five times. She has won at least one singles title a year from 2003 to 2015, a record bested only by three other female players—Steffi Graf, Martina Navratilova, and Chris Evert.

Off the court, Sharapova has worked as a model and has numerous lucrative product endorsement deals. She has her own tennis apparel collection—the Nike Maria Sharapova Collection—and a premium candy line called Sugarpova. She is also a United Nations Goodwill Ambassador, with a special focus on the UN's Chernobyl Recovery and Development Programme.

CHAPTER FIVE

GET IN THE GAME!

Tennis is an easy sport to try out and have fun with before deciding it's something you have a passion for and are skilled in. Most towns and cities have public courts, beginner's rackets are inexpensive, and no other special equipment or high-tech apparel is necessary. You don't even need to go to a court to play informally—you can just go out and hit a ball against a wall or volley with a friend. If the tennis bug bites you, and you want to pursue the game more seriously, your next step is probably taking lessons, attending camps, and joining school teams.

There are thousands of players all over the country participating in tennis camps, events, and tournaments for men and women of all ages. The United States Tennis Association has many different leagues for competitive tennis. There are even official USTA tournaments for players in their eighties and nineties

GET IN THE GAME!

There are many paths to becoming a tennis champ. If your school does not have a tennis program, try searching for local clubs you can join.

JUNIOR TENNIS

There are many junior programs all over the world that sponsor tennis tournaments, lessons, clinics, and camps for boys and girls ages eight to eighteen. The USTA has a competitive league called Junior Team Tennis. Junior Team Tennis is a fun way to meet other kids and play matches against one another. Many city recreation departments and YMCAs also have junior tennis leagues. Thanks to Title IX, today you can visit almost any high school in the United States and find a girls' tennis team. Just as in other sports, girls' tennis teams compete against teams from other schools in their division. A high school tennis team is usually composed of girls who compete in either singles or doubles play.

COLLEGE TENNIS

Many players decide that they would like to play tennis in college. Because of Title IX, there are many girls' tennis teams found on college and university campuses. If a girl played tennis well enough in high school, she may even attend college on a sports scholarship.

The level of coaching and playing ability varies from school to school. Southern California schools, for instance, employ strong coaches. In other areas of the country, tennis is not as popular or competitive a sport, making it easier to earn a spot on college tennis teams.

The schools in the National Collegiate Athletic Association (NCAA) are classified into three divisions. The most competitive teams are in Division I. There are a number of other college athletic associations, such as the National Association of Intercollegiate Athletics (NAIA) and the New England Small College Athletic Conference (NESCAC). The NESCAC's mission statement says

IT'S A LIVING!

Thanks to pioneers like Billie Jean King, professional women's tennis can be both an athletically and a financially rewarding profession. In 1974, Chris Evert was the first woman to make over a million dollars playing professional tennis. Today, most of the top women tennis professionals are multimillionaires from both tournament winnings and lucrative product endorsement and development deals with corporate sponsors.

Female professional players now compete for over $118 million a year in prize money. In recent years, as many as twenty-five players have won at least $1 million annually. In 2015, Maria Sharapova, despite losing her last seventeen matches against Serena Williams, was ranked as the highest paid woman in sports, thanks to her many endorsement deals. From June 2014 to June 2015, she earned $29.7 million, with only $6.7 million of that coming from prize earnings. Williams earned $24.6 million in that same period, with most of it coming from prize money.

that it is "committed first and foremost to academic excellence and believes that athletic excellence supports our educational mission."

THE SPORT OF A LIFETIME

On the recreational level, tennis is a wonderful way to make friends and stay in good physical condition. You can see entire families

TENNIS

Getting exercise and making friends are just some of the many reasons tennis has appealed to generations of males and females alike.

playing tennis together, couples enjoying themselves playing mixed doubles, and friends of many different ages joining USTA leagues. Tennis is truly a sport of a lifetime.

TIMELINE

1881 The U.S. Champion Tennis Tournament begins. In 1968, the name of the tournament is changed to the U.S. Open.

1884 Women's events are added to the Wimbledon tennis tournament.

1916 The American Tennis Association is formed. This is the oldest African American sports organization in the United States.

1927 Helen Wills Moody is the first American woman to win Wimbledon.

1935 The U.S. Champion Tennis Tournament officially includes women.

1947 Althea Gibson wins the first of ten consecutive American Tennis Association national championships.

1951 Gibson becomes the first African American to enter Wimbledon. She would later win Wimbledon twice.

1953 Maureen "Little Mo" Connolly, age sixteen, becomes the first woman to score a calendar-year Grand Slam (winning Wimbledon and the U.S., French, and Australian Opens within one calendar year).

1956 Gibson wins the French Open, becoming the first African American to win a Grand Slam singles title.

1971 The Association for Intercollegiate Athletics for Women is formed. Billie Jean King becomes the first female athlete to win more than $100,000 in a single season in any sport.

1972 King is named the Sportswoman of the Year by *Sports Illustrated*. The U.S. Congress passes Title IX of the Education Amendments of 1972.

TENNIS

1973 The U.S. Tennis Association announces that men and women will receive equal prize money at the U.S. Open.

1974 Chris Evert is named the Associated Press Female Athlete of the Year for tennis. She would win this distinction three more times.

1976 Evert becomes the first female athlete to record $1 million in career earnings.

1982 Martina Navratilova becomes the first woman to earn $1 million within a single season.

1984 Navratilova earns $2 million in a single season, more than the men's world number one at the time, John McEnroe.

1988 Tennis reappears at the Olympic Games for the first time since the 1928 Games. Steffi Graf wins the gold medal and becomes the second woman to achieve a calendar-year Grand Slam. Winning a gold medal and the calendar-year Grand Slam is known as a "Golden Slam."

1990 Navratilova wins a record ninth Wimbledon singles championship.

1997 Martina Hingis, at age sixteen and a half, becomes the youngest woman to win a major tennis tournament—the Australian Open—in 110 years.

1999 About sixty professional female tennis players sign a petition asking the WTA to award men and women equal prize money at all four Grand Slam tournaments.

2001 Venus Williams becomes a Grand Slam champion with her straight set win at Wimbledon over Lindsay Davenport. She is only the second African American women's champion in the history of Wimbledon.

2002 The Williams sisters both reach the world number one ranking, Venus in February and Serena in July.

TIMELINE

2003 Serena Williams completes a "Serena Slam"—winning four consecutive, non–calendar year Grand Slam tournaments.

2006 Martina Navratilova retires. During her thirty-two-year career, she set records for most singles titles (167) and most Wimbledon titles (nine). Her career singles record was 1,442-219, while her doubles record was 747-143.

2007 All four major tournaments—the U.S. Open, the French Open, the Australian Open, and Wimbledon—offer men and women equal prize money for the first time ever. Justine Henin becomes the first woman to earn $5 million in a single season.

2009 Thirteen finals are won by first-time champions, revealing the depth of talent in women's tennis.

2012 Maria Sharapova wins the French Open to earn a career Grand Slam (achieved by winning the U.S. Open, French Open, Australian Open, and Wimbledon at least once).

2013 The WTA, founded by Billie Jean King in 1973, recognizes four decades of growth and achievement with a season-long tribute to the pioneers of the game and the current stars who all contributed to the ongoing success of women's professional tennis and the WTA.

2015 Serena Williams wins four consecutive major titles from the 2014 U.S. Open through the 2015 Wimbledon, the second non–calendar year Grand Slam of her career. She was poised to become only the fourth tennis player to achieve a calendar-year Grand Slam if she won the 2015 U.S. Open, but she lost in the semifinals.

GLOSSARY

ALLEY LINE Inside vertical line on the tennis court; designates singles court.

BACKCOURT The area between the service line and the baseline.

BACKHAND A tennis stroke in which the ball is hit with the back side of the racket. The shoulder of the arm holding the racket faces the net before bringing the racket forward and across the body to meet the ball. If a player is right-handed, a shot hit on the left side of the player's body would be her backhand. For a left-hander, it would be a shot hit on her right side.

BASELINE The line at the back of the court.

BASELINE RALLY When both players stand at or behind the baseline to hit the ball back and forth to each other.

CROSSCOURT When a player hits the ball diagonally across the court, over the net. This is the highest percentage shot you can hit because the ball has to travel over the lowest part of the net for the longest distance on the court.

DEUCE Tied score of 40-40. Because a game must be won by two points, play continues until one player leads by a margin of two points.

DOUBLE FAULT Two consecutive serving errors that result in the loss of a point.

FOREHAND A tennis stroke in which the player pivots her body so that the shoulder of the arm not holding the racket faces the net. The player then swings the racket forward to meet the ball. The ball is hit on the right side on a player if she is right-handed, and the left side if she is left-handed.

GLOSSARY

GAME A tennis game is composed of at least four points. The winner must win by a margin of two points.

GROUNDSTROKE A tennis stroke generally hit by a player from the baseline.

HARD COURT Any tennis court that is made from an asphalt derivative or synthetic surface.

LOVE Term for a score of zero. This can pertain to points, games, and sets.

POINTS, GAMES, SETS, AND MATCHES Points make up games, games make up sets, and sets make up matches. When a player wins four points by a margin of two, she has won a game. When a player wins six games (with the exception of 5-all and 6-all), she has won a set. Most matches are best-of-three tiebreak sets. Someone must win two out of three sets to win the match. In some tournaments, men must win three out of five sets to win the match.

RALLY A series of shots hit back and forth between two players.

RECEIVER The player who receives the serve.

SERVE Begins every point of a tennis match. A player is allowed two tries to make a legal serve.

SERVICE BOX The rectangular area in which a legal serve must land. Also referred to as the service court.

SERVICE LINE The horizontal line 18 feet (5.5 m) from the baseline. It is the start of the service court.

VOLLEY A shot made before the ball bounces; often used by the player at the net.

For More Information

International Tennis Hall of Fame

194 Bellevue Avenue

Newport, RI 02840

(401) 849-3990

Website: https://www.tennisfame.com

As part of the global tennis community, the International Tennis Hall of Fame is committed to preserving tennis history, celebrating its champions, and educating and inspiring a worldwide audience. The Museum at the International Tennis Hall of Fame shares the narrative of tennis history from its origins through present day. It is split into three areas, *The Birth of Tennis (1874–1918)*; *The Popular Game (1918–1968)*; and *The Open Era (1968–Present)*.

Tennis Canada

Aviva Centre

1 Shoreham Drive, Suite 100

Toronto, ON M3N 3A6

Canada

(416) 665-9777

Website: http://www.tenniscanada.com

Founded in 1890, Tennis Canada is a nonprofit, national sport association responsible for leading the growth, promotion, and showcasing of tennis in Canada. Tennis Canada owns and operates two of the premier events of the ATP World Tour and WTA. In addition, Tennis Canada owns and operates eight professional ITF sanctioned events and financially

FOR MORE INFORMATION

supports eleven other professional tournaments in Canada. Tennis Canada operates junior national training centers/programs at the Centre of Excellence in Toronto, Uniprix Stadium in Montreal, and the North Shore Winter Club in Vancouver.

Tennis Professionals Association (TPA)
Website: http://www.tpacanada.com
TPA serves Canada's tennis professionals, including coaches and instructors. The organization offers courses, workshops, seminars, and provides other resources, including career services and information about clubs and scholarships.

United States Tennis Association (USTA)
70 West Red Oak Lane
White Plains, NY 10604
(914) 696-7000
Website: http://www.usta.com
The USTA is the national governing body for the sport of tennis and the recognized leader in promoting and developing the sport's growth on every level in the United States, from local communities to the crown jewel of the professional game, the U.S. Open.

Women's Sports Foundation
247 West 30th Street, Suite 7R
New York, NY 10001
(646) 845-0273
Website: http://www.womenssportsfoundation.org
Founded in 1974 by tennis legend Billie Jean King, the Women's Sports Foundation is dedicated to advancing the

lives of girls and women through sports and physical activity.

Women's Tennis Association (WTA)
Corporate Headquarters
100 Second Avenue South, Suite 1100-S
St. Petersburg, FL 33701
(727) 895-5000
Website: http://www.wtatennis.com
The WTA is the global leader in women's professional sport, with more than 2,500 players representing ninety-two nations competing for a record $129 million in prize money at the WTA's fifty-five events and four Grand Slams in thirty-three countries.

WEBSITES

Because of the changing nature of Internet links, Rosen Publishing has developed an online list of websites related to the subject of this book. This site is updated regularly. Please use this link to access this list:

http://www.rosenlinks.com/IX/Tennis

FOR FURTHER READING

Anniss, Matt. *Venus & Serena Williams in the Community*. New York, NY: Britannica Educational Publishing, 2014.

Bailey, Diane. *Venus and Serena Williams: Tennis Champions*. New York, NY: Rosen Central, 2010.

Blumenthal, Karen. *Let Me Play: The Story of Title IX: The Law that Changed the Future of Girls in America*. New York, NY: Atheneum Books for Young Readers, 2005.

Elliott, Bruce, Machar Reid, and Miguel Crespo. *Tennis Science: How Player and Racquet Work Together*. Chicago, IL: University of Chicago Press, 2015.

Flink, Steve. *The Greatest Tennis Matches of All Time*. Chicago, IL: New Chapter Press, 2012.

Hodgkinson, Mark. *Game, Set, and Match: Secret Weapons of the World's Top Tennis Players*. New York, NY: Bloomsbury USA, 2015.

Hoskins-Burney, Tina, and Lex Carrington. *Tennis Drill Book*. Champaign, IL: Human Kinetics, 2014.

Huss, Sally. *Eight Golden Rules for How to Play Your Best Tennis*. La Jolla, CA: Huss Publishing, 2012.

Mitchell, Kevin. *Break Point: The Inside Story of Modern Tennis*. London, England: John Murray, 2015.

Mitchell, Nicole. *Encyclopedia of Title IX and Sports*. Santa Barbara, CA: Greenwood, 2007.

Parsons, John, and Henry Wancke. *The Tennis Book: The Illustrated Encyclopedia of World Tennis*. London, England: Carlton Books, 2012.

Polishook, Rob. *Tennis Inside the Zone: 32 Mental Training Workouts for Champions*. Quebec City, QC: Smart Cat Publishing, 2015.

Roetert, Paul, and Mark Kovacs. *Tennis Anatomy*. Champaign, IL: Human Kinetics, 2011.

Ryan, Mike. *Tennis' Greatest Stars*. Richmond Hill, ON: Firefly Books, 2014.

Williams, Serena, with Daniel Paisner. *My Life: Queen of the Court*. New York, NY: Simon & Schuster, 2009.

Williams, Venus, with Kelly E. Carter. *Come to Win: Business Leaders, Artists, Doctors, and Other Visionaries on How Sports Can Help You Top Your Profession*. New York, NY: Amistad, 2010.

INDEX

A
Australian Open, 33, 38, 39, 44, 47

B
backhand, 16, 17, 18, 23, 27

F
forehand, 16, 17, 23
French Open, 33, 37, 38, 39, 43, 44, 47

G
Gibson, Althea, 36–37, 44
Grand Slam, 14, 31, 33, 38, 39, 44, 45, 46, 47

I
International Tennis Hall of Fame, 38, 43, 44

K
King, Billie Jean, 6–7, 31, 37–39, 51

L
Lenglen, Suzanne, 40–43

N
Navratilova, Martina, 39, 43–44, 45, 46, 47
Nelson, Mariah Burton, 31

O
Olympic Games, 35, 41, 45, 47

R
Riggs, Bobby, 7, 38

S
Sharapova, Maria, 7, 43, 46–47, 51

T
tennis
  apparel, 11, 42, 47, 48
  equipment, 7, 10–11, 35, 48
injuries, 11, 20, 22, 25–27
  court layout, 12–13
  lessons, 22, 25, 48, 50
  lingo, 23–24
scores, 11, 13–14, 23
serves and other shots, 14–18
training for, 19–27
Title IX, 4–7, 50

U
United States Tennis Association (USTA), 23, 38, 48, 50, 52
U.S. Open, 33, 35, 38, 39, 43, 44, 45, 47

W
Williams, Venus, 7, 43, 44–45
Williams, Serena, 7, 31, 33, 43, 44, 45, 46, 51
Wimbledon, 33, 35, 37, 39, 41, 44, 45, 46, 47
Women's Tennis Association (WTA), 7, 14, 38, 43, 44

ABOUT THE AUTHORS

Nita Mallick is a writer based in central New Jersey. She has played tennis recreationally since she was a teen and enjoys watching her favorite players compete in the Grand Slam tournaments each year.

Judith Guillermo-Newton is a psychotherapist who lives in Santa Barbara, California. She has been a recreational tennis player for much of her life and plays on a USTA tennis team. She is the mother of two daughters, both of whom played on their high school varsity tennis teams.

PHOTO CREDITS

Cover FikMik/Shutterstock.com; p. 5 Dennis Macdonald/Photolibrary/Getty Images; p. 9 Popperfoto/Getty Images; p. 10 C-You/iStock/Thinkstock; p. 12 Mike Price/Shutterstock.com; p. 15 Goran Bogicevic/Shutterstock.com; p. 17 Bob Thomas/E+/Getty Images; p. 21 Gerard Brown/Dorling Kindersley/Getty Images; p. 22 XiXinXing/Thinkstock; p. 25 Capifrutta/Shutterstock.com; p. 26 Alila Medical Media/Shutterstock.com; p. 29 Flashon Studio/Shutterstock.com; p. 30 Stan Honda/AFP/Getty Images; p. 32 Galina Barskaya/Shutterstock.com; p. 34 StockLite/Shutterstock.com; p. 36 Pool/Getty Images; p. 37 Folb/Hulton Archive/Getty Images; p. 38 © AP Images; p. 47 Frederic J. Brown/AFP/Getty Images; p. 49 LuckyBusiness/iStock/Thinkstock; p. 52 Digital Vision/Photodisc/Thinkstock; cover and interior pages graphic elements vector illustration/Shutterstock.com.

Designer: Nicole Russo; Editor: Shalini Saxena; Photo Researcher: Sherri Jackson